Published by
Enchanted Lion Books
201 Richards Street, Studio 4
Brooklyn, NY 11231

Text copyright © 2009 by Dirk Derom
Illustrations copyright © 2009 by Sarah Verroken

Typeset in P22 Garamouche Bold and Regular.
Designed by P22. P22 type foundry creates computer
typefaces inspired by Art, History, and sometimes Science.

[A CIP record is on file with the Library of Congress]

ISBN-978-1-59270-087-5

Printed by Schaubroeck nv, Belgium, on Munken print white, 150 gsm

PIGEON
Dirk Derom AND Sarah Verroken
PIGEONETTE

ENCHANTED LION BOOKS
New York

The woods are silent.

Not a breeze, nor a chirp.

Nothing but winter's cold

mantling the trees with snow.

All the birds have departed

for the sun and warm toes.

All but one,
whose little wings can carry her
no further then a foot.

Pigeonette will spend
her winter in the woods,
flapping her little wings
as she hops across the snow.

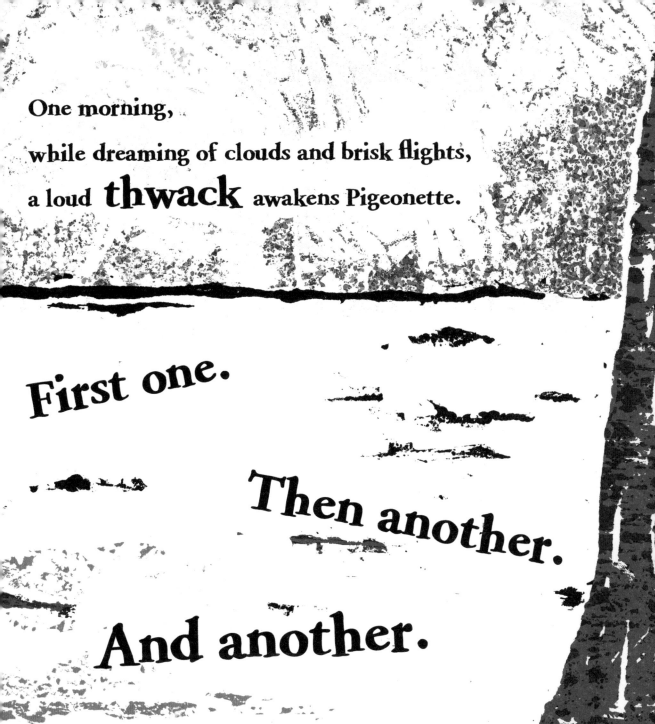

One morning,

while dreaming of clouds and brisk flights,

a loud **thwack** awakens Pigeonette.

First one.

Then another.

And another.

Looking up,

Pigeonette sees a **huge** bird,

climbing a **big** tree,

jumping and flapping his way up,

until he smacks

right into the trunk of

a towering oak.

"Dear Mr. Pigeon," says Pigeonette,

"why don't you like oaks?"

"It's not the oak, nor the birch, nor the lime tree

that I dislike," Pigeon replies with a sigh.

"It's just that it's always dark to these big eyes."

"It's sad when pigeons can't fly,"
muses Pigeonette.

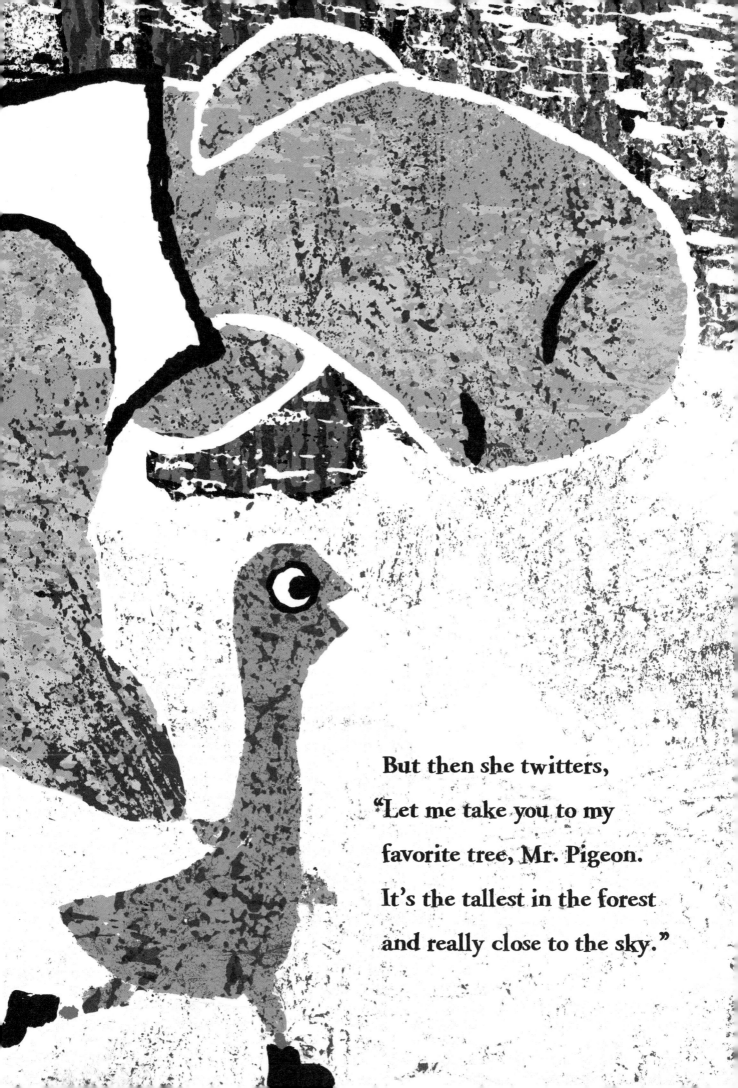

But then she twitters,
"Let me take you to my
favorite tree, Mr. Pigeon.
It's the tallest in the forest
and really close to the sky."

The two friends slowly climb
to the top of the highest oak
to talk about their dreams.

There, on Pigeonette's favorite branch,
the wind blows strongly
and for a moment they truly feel
as if they are flying.

"I want to soar higher than an eagle!"

shouts Pigeonette,

climbing onto Pigeon's shoulders.

"One day we will reach the clouds!"

Pigeon dreams aloud,

while Pigeonette hops excitedly.

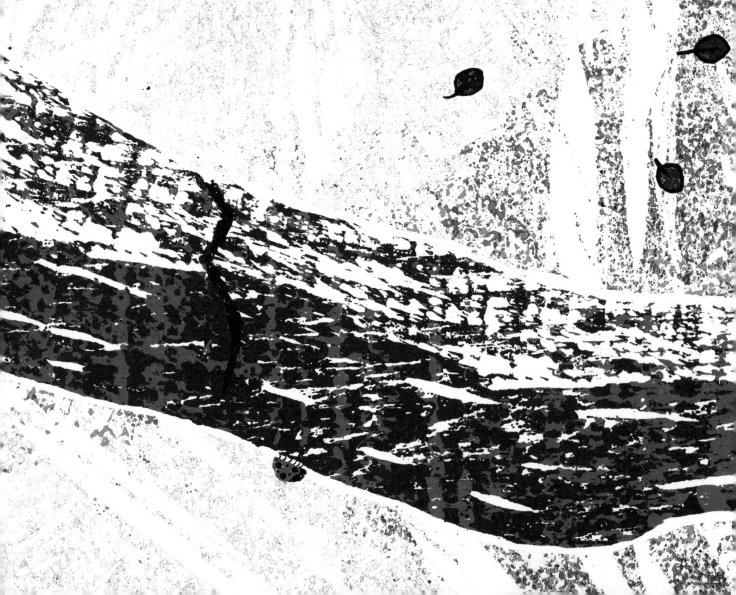

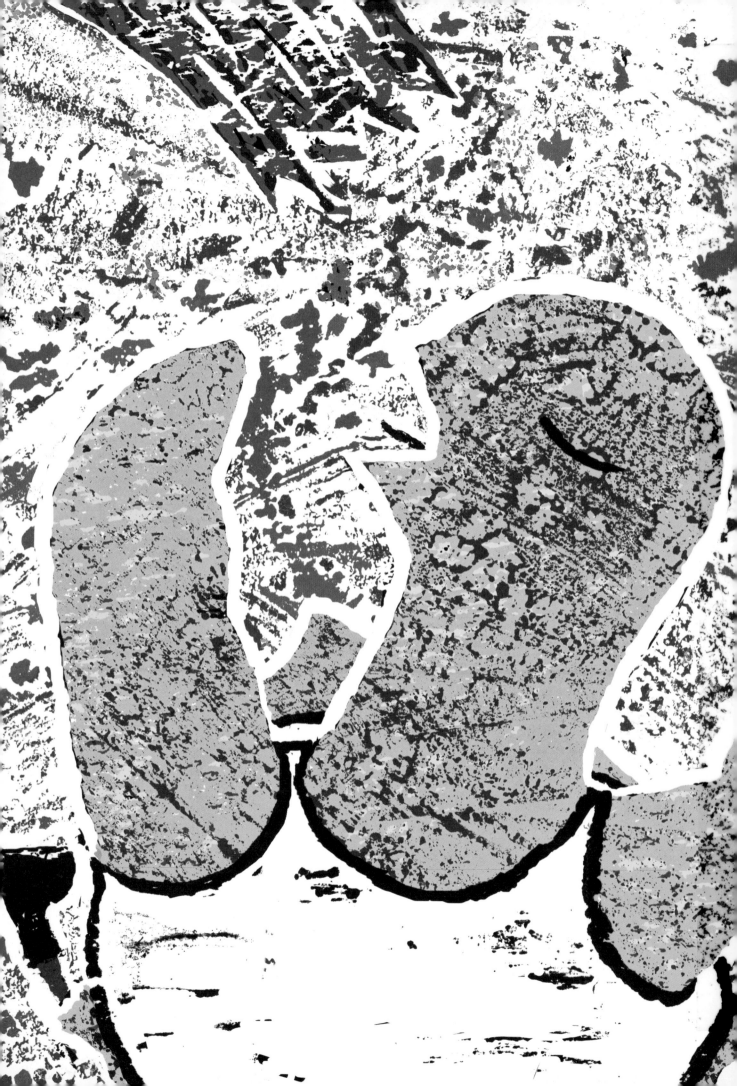

But Pigeon and Pigeonette
are too heavy,
and with her ninth hop,
the branch breaks.

"WAAAAAAW,

WOOOOOOW,"

our two friends cry
as they tumble down.

As they soar,
the wind wooshes
past their little ears.

"How high are we?" yells Pigeon.

"The trees look like green corngrains
and the cows small dots," Pigeonette replies:

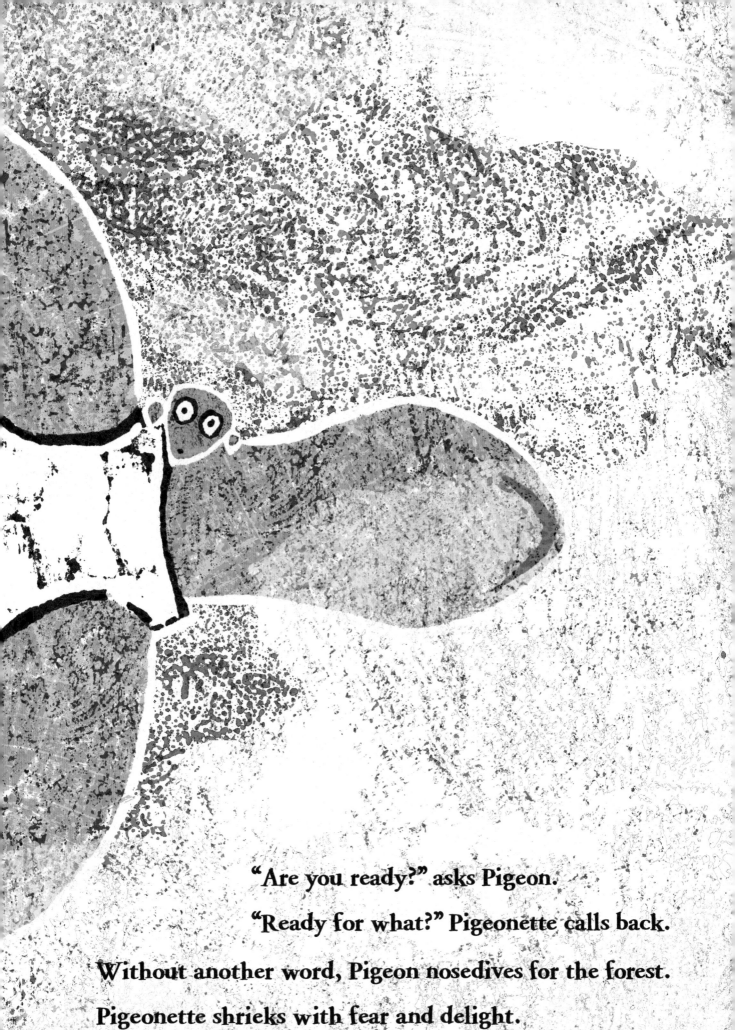

"Are you ready?" asks Pigeon.

"Ready for what?" Pigeonette calls back.

Without another word, Pigeon nosedives for the forest.

Pigeonette shrieks with fear and delight.

Back in the woods,

Pigeon stretches out his feet

preparing to land.

"It's too slippery!"

are the last words

out of the big wheeling snowball.

"We did it!" pants Pigeonette, breaking into a silly dance.

"Well done, Pigeonette! This time I felt the leaves of the oak,

but didn't hit its trunk!"

Pigeon says proudly.

Later that day,
both are asleep
with the biggest smile
a pigeon can have.

From then on,
all day long right through the summer,
the chirping voice of Pigeonette
guides Pigeon through the mighty forest.

Surely now and then,
after a wild flight,
they crash down with a big thump.

But they keep on trying
till they almost touch the moon.

From time to time,
they listen to the wise old pigeon Firmin,
who tells them the secret
of how to find their way home
when rainy storms and rolling thunder
rule the sky.

When summer is gone and autumn arrives,
Pigeon and Pigeonette are ready
to trade the woods for new horizons.

Carried by Pigeon's strong wings,
guided by Pigeonette's bright eyes,
they take off on their first trip
to warmer toes.

So next time in autumn,
when you are strolling
through the fields or in the park,
you might just catch a glimpse
of Pigeon and Pigeonette,

as they set off
with nibbles for the day,
crossing rivers and groves,
cities and farms,
to meet **the sun.**